A Warrenton Christmas Adventure

by
Katherine Eppley

Illustrations by Kellie Davies

Editor Nichole Brown

Tinsel Thyme Press

A Warrenton Christmas Adventure

©2023 by Tinsel Thyme Press LLC.,
Warrenton, Virginia

Manuscript © 2023 by Katherine Eppley
Illustrations © 2023 by Kellie Davies
Paperback version printed in 2023

Photo Credit – photograph taken by Travis Rogers
of Reformed Photography, Warrenton, Virginia.

ISBN 978-1-7347906-8-9
Library of Congress Control Number: 2023911517

Dedication

This book is dedicated to several people who have played important roles in bringing this book to life. James, Nichole, and Zechariah – Thank you for allowing me to "run" with the idea and for all your support with editing, publishing, and marketing! This would not have happened without you. It is fascinating to see how God brings all the pieces of the puzzle together from reaching out to James for help on a family matter to editing James' books to co-authoring a book with Nichole to writing *A Warrenton Christmas Adventure* – y'all have been such a tremendous blessing and such wonderful friends!

Thank you to my family – Eric, Brett, Brooks, Carter, and Emily! Y'all have done so much to support and encourage this dream of mine. You truly have no idea how much this has meant to me.

Thank you to my friends and extended family who have listened to me talk about this for months! I know I must have driven some of y'all crazy at times, but you all never wavered in your support.

Sharon Krasny – Thank you for being an inspiration to me.

Jess – Thank you for all your encouragement and reviewing the workout chapter for me! You are awesome!

Thank you, Kellie Davies, for your amazing illustrations which help bring the story to life!

Thank you also, to all who read this book! May you enjoy it as much as I enjoyed writing it!

Tinsel, a very junior elf with an impish nature, endless curiosity and an intense desire to prove himself brave and clever to his fellow elves, loves to stealthily listen at open doors wherever possible. Can you guess what Tinsel does after listening to Santa and Mrs. Claus?

Chapter 1: A Special Invitation

Melvin, the mail clerk, was an elf on a mission. He quickly maneuvered around all the elves busily making toys on his way to Santa's office. Inside, there was one particular elf reigned over the office. All the North Pole elves called this elf, Holly, the "Ruler of Santa's Office". Just as Melvin reached out to open Santa's office door, Holly exclaimed, "You cannot go in there! Santa is in conference with Mrs. Claus making the schedule for the holiday calendar for the North Pole. You know they have to review all the special event requests sent from around the world! Then they have to plan out all the details for a few quick international trips, just to be sure everything is ready for Christmas Eve."

"Then I have excellent timing," Melvin responded. "A few more special requests arrived this morning. They will need these immediately!"

"Well, in that case, knock 3 times, sing the first line of Feliz Navidad and open the door," declared Holly. "Then Santa will know this is an essential interruption and you may enter."

Santa Claus and his lovely wife, Mrs. Claus, looked up as Melvin entered the room. "What brings you here at this time of day?" asked Santa. "You always appear promptly at lunchtime with the day's mail."

"I noticed a few more special requests arrived today and thought you and Mrs. Claus would need them as you plan out the December schedules," Melvin replied.

"More invitations?" Santa laughingly replied. "I wish I could accept all the invitations sent to us every year, but we cannot be in multiple places at the same time. Not even a full reindeer team can fly that fast!"

"Well, Santa, I am sure that we can attend one or two of these special events at least. Let's see what came today," proclaimed Mrs. Claus. "Ah – here is one from a little town in Virginia, in Fauquier County. They have a tradition of welcoming Santa into town on the first Friday in December every year. You would ride on a fire engine through the parade! Next, you would - oh my – how fun! It seems that the town transforms one of the historic buildings in the center of town into a winter wonderland, decorated to give children an astounding experience. Gum Drop Square is the name of this magical place, where children eagerly await their turn to meet Santa. What a deliciously lovely event!"

"According to the calendar, we have not planned anything after Thanksgiving weekend yet. After all those televised parades, Santa, my dear, you know it would lift your spirits to see so much holiday cheer in a charming, quaint rural town. I, for one, would certainly enjoy going to Warrenton to participate in their Christmas parade!" suggested Mrs. Claus.

"Holly!" called Santa. "Please have Bernard, the Head Elf, stop by ASAP! Mrs. Claus and I will make a quick trip down south the week after Thanksgiving, and we need to review the schedules for gift production and the reindeer-in-training program."

Holly got on the North Pole intercom system immediately and called for Bernie (as everyone but Santa called Bernard) to report to Santa's office as fast as possible. As Bernie heard his name, he thought, "Wow! I know Santa and Mrs. Claus were discussing the holiday schedules today. They must have something really amazing they want to do! I'd better get there right now!" Yelling, "Make way! Move aside!", Bernie ran as quickly as he could through the crowd of elves who all suspected something exciting was in the works.

Noticing Bernie pulled up short at the office door, Mrs. Claus said, "Bernie – thank you for coming so quickly!" Her eyes sparkled with merriment as she continued, "Santa and I have a unique opportunity! The Town of Warrenton has invited us to join in their annual Christmas parade! Now, I will leave so you and Santa can get down to business. I must go pick out one of Santa's best suits for the occasion so he will look his finest for this special event."

Later, Santa, otherwise known as Kris Kringle, returned to his and Mrs. Claus' cozy and cheery home. He always enjoyed walking into the house, seeing how much love and attention his bride put into all the decorations. Mrs. Claus, also known by her first name, Jessica, prided herself on her unique collection of global treasures which featured Santa, the elves, gingerbread houses, and nutcrackers. On occasion when she got to travel with Kris, she delighted in shopping for pieces to add to her collections.

Earlier, as Mrs. Claus had made her way up to the climate-controlled room where all of Santa's suits and accessories were stored, she had wondered what she might discover in the shops which Warrenton's Mayor had mentioned in the invitation. Mrs. Claus quietly said to herself, "I would really like to find a new nutcracker or gingerbread house. It will be so much fun to look around in all the unique shops!"

Upstairs, Mrs. Claus sang her favorite carols as she inspected Santa's suits for any rips, frays, or holes. She also looked for any stains from the treats families left out for Santa on Christmas Eve. While Mrs. Claus checked Santa's most recent suit, Dexter, the Chief Tailor, and his crew were polishing up Santa's new boots and belt.

These highly skilled elves were responsible for the out-of-season storage, repair work and replacement of pieces too worn to repair, but Mrs. Claus always made the final inspections of her husband's famous apparel. After all, Dexter and Mrs. Claus both agreed that Santa should always look his absolute best when dressed formally in his Santa suit!

Mrs. Claus said, "Dexter, please pass along my deep appreciation for all the care your team takes with Santa's suits and accessories. All those chimneys take a toll on his clothes, but it is so important to maintain Santa's tip-top appearance in public! Children always notice the slightest smudge on Santa's boots or stain on his white gloves."

Once Mrs. Claus had finished her task, she called for Santa to come on up for the final fitting of his newest jacket and pants. While Dexter pinned the hem on Santa's pants, Mrs. Claus commented on how Dexter's precise detailed work always resulted in such perfectly fitted suits. Santa agreed, "Dexter, just like Mrs. Claus, I appreciate your dedication and skills. Your efforts make me look fantastic! Thank you!"

Dexter smiled as he replied, "It is truly an honor to be your Chief Tailor, Santa. I remember when I was a junior apprentice and was allowed in the room during one of your suit fittings. It was such an amazing privilege for a junior elf! I recall how I was so nervous I was literally shaking! The last century has sped by as I learned new skills, developing my abilities to match the extremely demanding level of expertise required of Santa's Official Chief Tailor. As the Tailor Shop motto says, 'Santa does not leave the North Pole until he is SEW PERFECT!' We are proud of our contribution in making Christmas the best and most delightful time of the year for everyone around the world."

Meanwhile, all of the North Pole reindeer were in training for Christmas Eve, when Santa needed them in tip-top condition. As you all know, the Official Team has to make it all the way around the world, stopping for every single child on the Nice List in one night. Santa, Fred and Ethel, the Head Veterinarians, along with Speedy, the Head Reindeer Coach, reviewed the cut-off requirements for the Official Team. While individual reindeer could fly faster than the others, the team had to work together to conserve energy and fly smoothly. It would never do to have Santa fall out of the sleigh just because a reindeer decided to show off!!

Official Team Requirements:

Minimum flying speed of 650 feet per second

Smooth starts and stops

Ability to avoid obstacles in mid-air

Match speeds with the rest of the team

Steady flight with efficient energy conservation

Ability to take and follow directions

Of course, only the best of the best could meet the Official Team Requirements. Speedy encouraged the remaining reindeer, saying, "You all gave the team tryouts your best effort! Santa and I are quite pleased with how well you did and want you to be proud of yourselves, too. We will meet with those of you who came close to meeting the requirements. All of you with solid potential should join the Junior Team. Your responsibilities will include working hard at team training exercises to improve your performance, attending multiple appearances at special events and preparing to serve as a substitute when needed for the Official Team."

The reindeer who had been disappointed only moments before, now happily smiled exclaiming, "Thank you, Coach Speedy! We are so happy that we can be of service to you, Santa! It was such a disappointment not to make the Official Team, but this gives us a way to increase our abilities, while still feeling like we are part of the North Pole team." Then the Junior Team and Official Team reindeer all followed the assistant coaches over to the meeting areas, so they could discuss training schedules.

Simultaneously, Santa, Fred, Ethel and Speedy moved to a quiet spot to discuss a few details regarding the Official Team. As Santa listened closely, the Head Veterinarians and Head Reindeer Coach all agreed that Dasher was almost at peak speed, 697 feet per second. Dancer had hit speeds close to his personal best of 656 feet per second. Fred and Ethel told Speedy and Santa that Dancer's love of Latin salsa dancing had effectively strengthened his hips and Prancer's yoga routines added strength and flexibility to his joints, so both reindeer were highly likely to hit new personal best speeds this season. Blitzen happened to be standing nearby overhearing all the training comments. He realized he was going to have his work cut out to keep his status as the second fastest reindeer on the team!

Did you guess that Tinsel would be so bold and brash to try and tag along on this adventure? He certainly is willing to risk getting caught by Santa to satisfy his curiosity about a small rural town called Warrenton!

Chapter 2: A Sprint and a Spring and Off They Go!

On the first Friday in December, even though it was before dawn, several elves volunteered to carry the bags including Santa's spare suit and Mrs. Claus' special cookies out to the sleigh, where the Official Team of reindeer were waiting excitedly. Santa spoke with the Head Reindeer Veterinarians, Fred and Ethel, to be sure all was well with the team. In just a few weeks these reindeer would fly Santa around the

world on Christmas Eve! He did not want to take any chances with the reindeer's health, so Fred and Ethel evaluated each of the nine reindeer. Luckily, the veterinarians cleared the team to travel.

Not a single team member wanted to miss out on this adventure. It would only take 24 minutes to fly from the North Pole to Warrenton, Virginia! The best part would be that they could actually meet some of the children who were usually snuggled up warm in their beds during Christmas Eve delivery runs.

Since this was an international flight, Santa had already filed his flight plan notifying all the aviation officials in Canada and the USA of the day, time, route, and altitude levels for this trip from the North Pole to Warrenton, Virginia. Santa finished uploading the official authorization from the USDA giving permission for the reindeer to travel in the USA.

As usual, flight controllers required Santa to acknowledge any instructions with his call sign of SleighRider1 and keep his KC25 transponder code activated at all times so the sleigh showed up on international radar systems. This way there would be no worry about such a fast-moving object in the sky because the air controllers would clear all planes from coming anywhere close to Santa and his reindeer.

With the North Pole air controllers granting flight clearance from North Pole International Travel, Santa gathered the reins in his hands and called for the reindeer to taxi down the NPIT departure lane.

As they lined up on the runway, the team leader called the team to take-off stance. Mrs. Claus held on tight to her harness as the reindeer sprinted down the lane, springing up into the air to launch the sleigh. She relaxed as the sleigh gained height and momentum, smoothly flying into the pre-dawn moonlight.

Santa looked over at his beloved wife and gently smiled, saying, "Take-off is always the best part! I need to remember to take you on more training flights, so you get used to the feeling when the team launches into the air. It's simply so exhilarating!"

Mrs. Claus responded, "My dear, I may be hanging on for dear life, but I do actually get a thrill when the team sprints down the lane and springs into the air. However – I would be happy to go on more of the training flights, anytime."

As planned, Santa and Mrs. Claus would arrive in time to do post-flight checks on the reindeer, set up the alarm system for the sleigh, meet with the parade organizers and have a chance to relax before the start of all the festivities. They enjoyed getting to see unique things and meet new people, especially Mrs. Claus! This was a rare opportunity for her to leave the North Pole because she simply had so many duties to oversee there on a daily basis. In addition, whenever Santa was away, she stepped up as the acting authority in charge of the North Pole.

For this short adventure, Bernie had been placed in temporary command. Santa and Mrs. Claus could not think of the last time Bernie had been so ecstatically happy: "I promise to keep to the production schedule while you are gone, Santa. No slacking off from any elf in any department!" Bernie declared upon being entrusted with such immense authority.

Rudolph, Dasher, Dancer, Prancer, Vixen, Comet, Cupid, Donner, and Blitzen took in all the sights as they glided high above Virginia. They beheld the stunning beauty of the Appalachian Mountains as the sun arose with glimpses of the Atlantic Ocean far off on the eastern coastline. With his booming bass voice, Donner led the team in singing Cupid's favorite Christmas carol, "Joy to the World." Ever the gentlemanly reindeer, Donner declared that Mrs. Claus should have the next choice of songs. Then, Blitzen, with his amazing tenor voice, sang a duet with Donner. As the team started to slowly descend, the singing came to an end so the team could focus on their final approach.

Mrs. Claus gazed at the blue-colored haze over the Blue Ridge Mountains while Santa announced they were about to arrive. He got on the radio to ask for landing clearance through Vint Hill TRACON (Terminal Radar Approach Control), who instantly recognized his SleighRider1 call sign and KC25 transponder code. Part of Santa's flight plan required him to avoid landing at an airport since airports are not usually equipped to handle Santa's sleigh or the nine reindeer. So, after confirming clearance to land, Santa pulled the team to a stop at the Fauquier County Fairgrounds just after sunrise.

The Mayor of Warrenton eagerly greeted Santa and Mrs. Claus, suggesting Santa park the sleigh inside the barn at the Fairgrounds. He then invited the reindeer to take advantage of the hay, snacks, and water while they rested after their journey. Graciously welcoming his VIP guests, the Mayor offered his profuse thanks for accepting the invitation to the Warrenton Christmas Parade.

Mrs. Claus thanked the Mayor for the lovely invitation. Santa praised the Mayor for the choice of landing site which provided a private shelter, water, and food for the reindeer. Additionally, Santa expressed his appreciation for being able to hide the sleigh away from anyone wanting to get a close look at it! He pointed out that only specially trained elves with high level security clearances were allowed to work on Santa's sleigh.

Can you believe Tinsel? While the others were chatting, Tinsel stealthily climbs into the back end of the Mayor's SUV so he can hitch a ride into town. He wants to discreetly follow Santa and Mrs. Claus to find out why Warrenton is so special.

Chapter 3: Zero to Sixty in a Split Second

As Santa and Mrs. Claus continued chatting with the Mayor, the reindeer started talking about all the things they had seen while flying into view of Fauquier County. They were excited about the speedway, farms, orchards and a number of lakes and parks. As the team tried to create a game plan for checking out various activities and locations, the reindeer started bickering over what to do first. Santa raised his voice, to make himself heard over top of the commotion: "Stop all that bickering! This is a quick trip to lift holiday spirits, so take care of your training and then go have fun! There is no need to bicker and argue, just draw straws to decide what comes first."

Santa continued in his normal, more gentle voice: "You have all morning and most of the afternoon until I need you to meet me at the old Mosby House on Main Street. Just please remember - we need to check in with the parade coordinator at 4:30pm."

Hopping into the Mayor's car, Santa and Mrs. Claus drove over to Main Street to have a bite of breakfast at one of the many wonderful places in town. There, they would meet the parade organizers to review the plans for Santa, Mrs. Claus, and the reindeer. After breakfast, Santa and Mrs. Claus began their adventure by exploring the unique and historical shops and buildings in Old Town Warrenton.

Once Santa and Mrs. Claus had left the Fairgrounds, the reindeer wandered around the fields at the Fairgrounds before deciding what to do first. The reindeer's head coach, Speedy, had sent specific workout plans to Kim, the friendly owner at a gym located just a hop-skip away from the Fairgrounds, called Old Town Athletic Campus (OTAC). Kim, and all the personal trainers were so excited for this once-in-a-lifetime opportunity to work with Santa's Official Reindeer Team! Jess, one of the experienced trainers, had set up a special area for the reindeer to work on starts, sprints and springs. She knew from the reindeer's Head Coach that this was a key part of reindeer training because it was tiring to be constantly taking off from one house to another house. Fridays were set aside specifically at the North Pole for these workouts. Landing skills were practiced on alternate days.

As the reindeer approached the gym, they saw a blonde-haired lady waving at them. After the team landed, she introduced herself to the team. "Hello! My name is Kim. I am one of the founders and owners of OTAC. Allow me to introduce Jess, one of our awesome trainers, and the rest of our training crew. We are all so excited to have you here today and to do whatever we can to support you and your Coach. Jess has the starting blocks and sprinting lanes ready based on your Coach's plan. Let's do this!"

Once the OTAC trainers made sure the reindeer completed each drill in Coach Speedy's workout plan, Jess collected up the trainers' notes to write up progress reports for Speedy, the Head Reindeer Coach. On behalf of the whole reindeer team, Rudolph thanked Kim, Jess, and the other trainers for hosting their training workout.

(Now many people may not realize this, but Rudolph has grown up quite a bit from the shy young reindeer he once was, into the confident team leader he is today. He really enjoys talking and being in the spotlight!) So, continuing on, Rudolph gratefully said, "Thank you all so much for your help in running our workout! All of you gave us great tips which will improve our take-off skills. Who knew that we would have so much in common with track athletes? All of us realize how consistent training will help us maintain peak flying speeds. Even Mrs. Claus keeps an eye on our training progress! It is absolutely imperative for us to be at our best because Santa trusts us to help him deliver all the gifts and not miss a single child on the Nice List anywhere in the world!"

Rudolph resumed, "Jess – Did you know you and Mrs. Claus share the same first name? In fact, you both have similar traits as well: strong leadership, kindness, gentle but firm and a great sense of humor. Both of you have the ability to adapt quickly as needed, motivate and encourage. We want to thank Jess, the entire trainer crew and Kim!"

Jess' smile stretched from ear to ear as she replied, "Thank you! I feel so honored you see similarities between Mrs. Claus and me. You have all done a great job today! Each of you had no trouble whatsoever in getting off the starting block and up to sixty mph in a split second – that kind of speed is just amazing! Keep up the good work! All of us at OTAC really enjoyed getting to assist you and your Coach. Thank you for letting us be a part of Operation Christmas Eve!"

All nine reindeer responded to Jess' praise with blushing smiles. Rudolph spoke up on their behalf: "Of course, Jess! Thank you again Kim and to all your training crew! We hope to see you all at the parade tonight – Merry Christmas!"

Kim, Jess and the training crew all eagerly declared: "We can't wait to see y'all tonight!"

Having finished their training workout, Dasher and Dancer suggested returning to the Fairgrounds barn so they could rest for a bit. After the team relaxed for a while, Comet and Cupid proposed they scout out the area more carefully. Since they had been rushing this morning and were also always in such haste on Christmas Eve, the reindeer readily agreed. Vixen dragged his heels a bit because he wanted a longer nap. Prancer and Rudolph eventually managed to get Vixen to go, so they all took to the sky to leisurely fly over and around Warrenton.

As you can see, Tinsel loves to take selfies! He is counting on these pictures as proof of his bravery as a stowaway on this adventure. Wonder what else he will discover in town?

Chapter 4: Discovering Old Town

Meanwhile, Santa and Mrs. Claus were enjoying a lovely cup of hot chocolate from an interesting little coffee shop, where they could watch people walking by on Main Street. As they sipped the silky-smooth hot chocolate, the Mayor introduced the parade organizers who thanked Santa for coming to Warrenton. Santa commented, "Getting to participate in local Christmas traditions such as the Warrenton Christmas Parade brings me so much joy! I am thrilled with the opportunity of riding on a fire truck, greeting all the children and their families."

Mrs. Claus jumped in, saying, "Having the chance to be one of your parade judges is definitely a highlight of this Christmas season for me! Santa and I both are so happy to be here today."

After the brief meeting, Santa and Mrs. Claus also managed to get a delicious breakfast sandwich from a little pop-in shop. Santa commented, "There are so many restaurants mixed in with such diverse shops! This breakfast sandwich is simply scrumptious and filling. Jessica, would you take a picture of it so we can see if our head chef can whip up something similar for us?"

Mrs. Claus exclaimed, "That is an excellent idea, Kris! I would love to have something like this for breakfast, especially on one of our crazy busy days at the North Pole!"

Mrs. Claus then spotted a few shops where she wanted to browse, so she and Santa entered the local specialty bakery, tasting the wonderful samples and purchased some delicious breads to share with Holly, Bernie, and Melvin back home. Upon leaving the bakery, Santa and Mrs. Claus visited the independent bookstore next door. Santa was pleasantly surprised to see there was a shelf dedicated to local authors and delighted to see so many holiday books for all ages. They found several books and magazines to enjoy reading at home after Christmas. Post-Christmas reading marathons were one of the most popular ways to relax after the busy weeks of December.

Next, they browsed through the local music store, impressed with its variety of quality instruments. The employee told them about the recent holiday music recital for their students. Santa and Mrs. Claus looked at each other as she said, "Oh Santa! I wish we could have attended the recital. I love to encourage music students by going to their recitals where they show what they have learned."

Santa adored how his wife loved supporting children and even adults who wanted to learn new skills. Thanking the employee, Santa offered his arm to Jessica and walked back out onto the brick sidewalk. Strolling along Main Street they noticed the lovely wreaths and Christmas decorations in the store windows and on the lamp posts.

Santa watched workers hurriedly set out the arrangements for the evening festivities. Parade volunteers were checking where the parade judges would sit, marking the spot for the first float in the lineup and putting signs in place warning parents to watch that their children didn't run out in front of parade vehicles.

A young man came running up to a lady who was holding a clipboard. He relayed a last-minute problem from one of the float groups. Apparently, the group's truck had a dead battery so they might be a bit late getting into place. The group leader was trying to locate another vehicle capable of safely pulling their trailer but needed help.

The lady calmly looked over her notes and swapped placements so another float could take the earlier spot, which would let the first group have more time to resolve the problem and still get to participate. She suggested a name and number for the young man to call about a possible replacement vehicle. He took off immediately, calling as he went, looking much relieved.

Santa commented to Mrs. Claus, "This town really takes their parade and festivities extremely seriously! I am impressed by all the organization, double-checking and trouble shooting. You were right once again my dear! I am very glad we decided to come down to Warrenton."

Continuing on down the street, Santa and Mrs. Claus came to another intriguing shop. As they browsed, both of them were fascinated by the tremendous variety of hand-made items throughout this international fair-trade store. Mrs. Claus strolled around the store, pleasantly enchanted by all that she saw. There were just so many things which would fit in well with her extraordinary collections in both her North Pole home and Santa's office. Every single item in her collections brought back special memories.

Mrs. Claus delightedly exclaimed, "Santa, dear, just look at these intricately made Christmas ornaments! We simply must take some of these home for our family tree."

Santa responded, "Of course! We should add some of these to our collection of unique ornaments, too. I hope you don't mind if we get another Nativity set as well. These olive wood Nativity sets are simply stunning!"

Upon leaving the shop, Santa and Mrs. Claus looked at the multiple bags holding the many items purchased for themselves, as well as many gifts for the elves. "What a lovely shop! With what we just bought, we are almost done now with our Christmas gift shopping," declared Mrs. Claus.

"We have had so much fun discovering all these shops featuring local authors, baked goods, jewelry, artwork, hand-made items, clothing, furniture, and that one-of-a-kind vanilla developed by the local pharmacist! Warrenton has so much to see, just here in Old Town" continued Mrs. Claus. Then she very quietly said to herself, "Sometime, I would very much enjoy seeing more of the whole county! I'll have to work on how to approach Santa about scheduling time to come back to this wonderful place."

Santa smiled saying, "I am so glad I brought my small magical bag I use in case of emergencies today! We need it to hold all of our wonderful purchases! This is so much easier than carrying all these bags." He started to pack away the latest gifts. Then Santa whispered to himself: "I would like to see what my wife would think about spending more time here in this lovely town and getting to explore the whole county."

Abruptly, realizing that there would not be time to eat dinner later, Santa and Mrs. Claus decided to have a bigger meal mid-afternoon. That would tide them over until arriving back at the North Pole, where they could munch on some of the delicious snacks they had picked up from Warrenton's various bakeries and quaint specialty shops. Mrs. Claus looked forward to the fruit cobbler bread, the macaroons, tin-plated pies, and unique cupcakes.

For now, though, they wanted to check out a few of the restaurants for their late lunch. They were having a difficult time deciding on whether they wanted to eat at a casual place or have a more formal meal. "Too many decisions to make," lamented Santa. "I would love to try out all of these eateries! Well, what do you think Jessica? Should we go for the casual place and just relax while we eat?"

"I agree," said Mrs. Claus, "Let's go and relax over a casual meal." Once they reviewed the menu, Mrs. Claus selected a salad with grilled chicken, while Santa chose a tasty pasta dish with garlic bread.

"Just please make sure to put on the oversize bib to protect your best suit while you eat! Tomato sauce does not look good on that white fur trim, not to mention trying to get that out of your beard!" teased Mrs. Claus. Santa smiled somewhat sheepishly as he recalled how hard it was to clean up after spilling anything on his beard and suit.

After enjoying their meal and being able to rest for a bit, Mrs. Claus and Santa realized there wasn't much free time left. "Wonder what the reindeer are doing," mused Santa. "Not to worry, I'm sure they are having fun," stated Mrs. Claus.

As Santa and Mrs. Claus started walking again, they noticed a rather colorful mural painted on the corner of Main Street and 2nd Street. "Greetings from Old Town" was spelled out using seven pictures depicting life around Warrenton for "Old Town". They both pulled out their phones to take selfies next to the mural. "What a fun way to create a postcard keepsake for our scrapbooks!" Mrs. Claus exclaimed. Santa posed in a goofy style, while Mrs. Claus took the photos.

During this time, the reindeer team had picked up enough speed that they could fly over the 650 square miles of Fauquier County within minutes. With the reindeer's exceedingly good eyesight, the team quickly spied out places they had noticed during their early morning flight: orchards out in Linden, the lake at Crockett Park, the speedway in Sumerduck, the museum in Goldvein, parks in Marshall and Great Meadows, for starters. The reindeer slowed to land in a secluded spot at Crockett Park. Dasher was all for immediately visiting the speedway, while Cupid wanted to check out the orchards and Donner strongly argued for going into a museum. However, Comet pointed out that there was simply not enough time to check out all the things they would like to do. An idea started to form amongst the team.

Blitzen asked the team to gather 'round and suggested, "What if we go talk with Mrs. Claus about this crazy, wonderful idea? If we can get her on our side before surprising Santa with this plan, Mrs. Claus will help us get Santa's approval. Otherwise - you know how careful Santa is about all of us going anywhere out of the North Pole." The other reindeer wholeheartedly agreed with Blitzen.

"Dancer, you are elected to speak for us with Mrs. Claus," declared Donner. "You do express ideas clearly. Besides, you always manage to stay on her good side since you're her favorite dance partner."

Before they could act on their plan, Blitzen, being such a dependable sort of reindeer, reminded the team that they were due to meet up with Santa very shortly. Following Blitzen's lead, they all turned to head back into the town. The reindeer did a low approach to land behind a beautiful church, so as not to attract too much attention.

As they wandered up Main Street, they spotted Santa and Mrs. Claus standing next to a wall on the corner of 2nd Street and Main Street. The reindeer laughed when they saw Santa taking silly selfie-style photos with a brightly colored mural! The team decided to take selfies, too.

While Mrs. Claus happily snapped photos, Santa asked the team, "How did it go with the training workout this morning? Did you all enjoy working out with the trainers there? I bet it was a nice break from working with Speedy and his assistant coaches! I hope you had a good rest and then took a look around Fauquier County this afternoon."

The reindeer all assured Santa they had finished the workout having a great time with the OTAC training crew. Dasher added, "Jess did an amazing job at setting up space for the team to complete all of what Coach Speedy had planned for us. We all enjoyed resting at the Fairgrounds barn and then exploring Fauquier County."

What the reindeer did not say is that they wanted to chat with Mrs. Claus about an idea for a vacation.

Prancer and Vixen chimed in to ask how Santa and Mrs. Claus had spent their day and what had been their favorite part of the trip so far. "Well," said Santa, "We have enjoyed meeting people as we went through many of the shops and seeing how well the town has prepared for their annual Christmas parade."

Mrs. Claus agreed, her eyes twinkling as she said, "So far Santa has definitely enjoyed all the food options. But we do wish we had time to take in more of the history and go inside the iconic Fauquier County Courthouse and Old Jail!"

At that, the reindeer smiled, realizing Dancer would easily be able to persuade Mrs. Claus to join in on their vacation dreams.

Tinsel has quietly climbed up a lamp post where he can see all that is happening on Main Street. He has never experienced so much holiday spirit! After all, Tinsel had never been outside of the North Pole before this adventure. What do you think - is this trip more than he could ever have imagined it would be?

Chapter 5: Time for the Parade!

By this time, the parade participants were starting to line up. All three high school marching bands took their places. The musicians had decorated their instruments with strands of Christmas lights and garland and were now warming up with holiday carols. The Junior ROTC, Girl Scouts and Boy Scouts unfurled flags and banners and checked their uniforms wanting to look their very best. Volunteers carefully drove special vehicles into position and then added last-minute signs and decorations onto the vehicles for the Mayor of Warrenton, Miss Fauquier County, Miss Teen Fauquier County, and other VIPs. Dance and cheer squads of all ages warmed up by stretching and dancing to the multiple sound systems and bands blasting out holiday music. Church groups, private schools, and other organizations, like the Fauquier SPCA and 4-H, loaded up onto pre-decorated floats or into the beds of pickup trucks.

The Mayor, who had been strolling through the crowds lining up along Main Street, saw Santa and Mrs. Claus. Knowing Mrs. Claus was due at the Judges/VIP stand at the Old Town Post Office, the Mayor guided her to the right spot. Mrs. Claus then met the rest of the judges who explained her special duties as a guest judge. After Mrs. Claus was all set, one of the parade organizers helpfully pointed out where Santa's ride was staged. So, Santa and the Mayor started walking in that direction, wandering through the parade groups, with Santa waving and saying "Ho, Ho, Ho." The reindeer team trailed along, enjoying people's reactions to Santa's greetings and to seeing nine real-live reindeer.

As they walked, the Mayor explained to Santa that the parade organizers had traditionally recruited a local farmer to furnish an old-fashioned wooden wagon filled with hay for folks to enjoy hayrides up and down Main Street after the parade. Years ago, there had been a small Friday evening parade when Santa rode into town on a hay wagon to open Gum Drop Square, where children could visit with Santa, plus a rather large Saturday morning parade for all the bands and organizations.

Earlier at the breakfast meeting, the Mayor had explained that a few years ago the parades were combined into one massive parade. At that time, the parade organizers decided to have Santa ride on a fire truck instead.

However, since children tremendously enjoyed riding up and down Main Street in the old-fashioned hay wagon, the organizers had decided to keep it as part of the Christmas Parade experience.

As they meandered along, Comet spotted something on the side of a building. He asked Rudolph and Dasher if they could tell what it was, but they shook their heads, saying, "No." Santa wondered what was holding up the team, so he walked right on over to the building to resolve the mystery. There they saw incredibly detailed murals which showed the town and its people in the 1860s. After looking at the paintings, the team turned into the next street to avoid the crowds on Main Street.

To their amazement, there stood an actual caboose, parked on railroad ties! The reindeer were delighted with this discovery and even more so, that the caboose was red.

They all asked to get another round of selfie-photos, but Santa reminded them, "We don't have much time left before the start of the parade! I know you want to read the information signs and check out the caboose, but I need to get to the fire truck without further delays. You all can take the time for one quick selfie shot, but then you've got to move quickly to meet me at the fire truck!"

The reindeer were a bit disappointed, but understood the time crunch. They looked knowingly at each other, and grinned. Blitzen quietly spoke, "I will be sure to talk with Mrs. Claus about our idea as soon as I can!"

Meanwhile, the Warrenton Volunteer Fire Department firefighters had decorated their Wagon 1 fire truck for Santa so he could safely sit up high enough on the truck for all to see him throughout the parade. Santa would be able to wave with both hands, so as not to disappoint the children who would be on both sides of the street. Additionally, the firefighters all said it was such a special privilege for them to personally drive Santa in the parade. Santa said, "I am honored to ride on your fire truck! First responders always have my utmost respect."

By now, the entire reindeer team caught back up with Santa. He was admiring Wagon 1, with the crew explaining how each part of the fire truck worked to help them effectively fight fires. Santa was fascinated by all the things the Wagon 1 fire truck could do. "Maybe," thought Santa, "I will suggest that the North Pole Emergency Response Team take a good look at getting one for the North Pole Fire Department. This could be rather helpful if we ever have an emergency."

Just then a parade organizer passed word that the Town of Warrenton police motorcycles and a Fauquier County Sherriff vehicle had started moving down the parade route. The first group was moving forward, so the parade had officially begun!

Everyone at the rear of the parade hurriedly moved into place, including the reindeer who were going to walk beside the fire truck. Santa climbed up on top of the fire truck with the help of the firefighters. He recalled Mrs. Claus' reminder to check that his hat was on just right, to adjust his red coat and to pull on his white gloves so as the fire truck went by the children could better see him wave.

While Santa prepared for the start of the parade, Mrs. Claus sat chatting with the other parade judges in the VIP/Judges viewing stand. Mrs. Claus explained, "We have several competitions up at the North Pole among the elves and the reindeer. Everyone has a fun time, athough the elves take the competitions so seriously. At times, they become a bit too serious, so we have to lighten things up a bit. From what I've seen so far, I am guessing that each of the float groups here have fun designing their floats while remaining highly competitive with the other groups." The judges commented that, "We have observed a competitive spirit in years past, but everyone does indeed have fun and always remembers the whole point is to celebrate Christmas."

Subsequently, the judges explained the three traditional awards: Most Original, Clarke Griswald and Judges' Choice. The first award was for the most creative in design and execution. The Griswald award was for the most over-the-top float, while the third award was for the float that they believed should be honored but didn't match the criteria for either of the first two awards.

However, this year they had decided to have a fourth award: Most Holiday Spirit. Since Mrs. Claus truly was a role model of holiday spirit, the judges asked her to hand out this new award. She replied, "I am truly honored to hand out this special award for Most Holiday Spirit, but it will be extremely difficult to choose just one winner!"

Just as Mrs. Claus had predicted, every float and group that paraded past the viewing stand proudly displayed their holiday spirit. All manner of music, costumes, dancing and lights shone out for all to see, bringing forth cheers and applause all the way down Main Street. Mrs. Claus thoroughly enjoyed all the parade participants' and the crowd's reactions. At the end of the parade, Mrs. Claus glowed with happiness. There was a special twinkle in her eye as she heard her husband shouting, "Merry Christmas, Merry Christmas to all"! She loved the way Santa made sure to notice every child along the parade route. She knew he was enjoying this event every bit as much as she was!

The idea which had started to take form earlier that day now solidified into an actual plan, and she smiled, thinking of how she would explain it to Santa later, on their way home to the North Pole. She believed her plan would be a fun surprise for Santa and the reindeer. Little did she know that Santa also had the same idea and so did the reindeer!

Once Santa rode past the viewing stand, signifying the parade's end, the judges quickly consulted their notes and voted on the first three awards. There was no question on Most Original or on the Clarke Griswald awards. It took a moment to discuss the top candidates for the Judges' Choice award, but that too, was decided unanimously.

In regard to the newest award, Mrs. Claus told her fellow judges that as expected, she could not simply give "Most Holiday Spirit" to just one group. Instead, she asked for their approval to have multiple winners. The judges agreed that since it was such a difficult decision, Mrs. Claus could announce as many winners as she liked.

At this point, the judges all walked over to the Fauquier County Courthouse. The awards were always handed out during the Christmas Tree Lighting Ceremony on the Courthouse steps. Parade observers and participants were already gathering at the steps, singing Christmas carols. The judges, the Mayor, Santa, and Mrs. Claus all stood at the top of the Courthouse steps. As the Mayor called for quiet, the parade organizers thanked everyone for coming and then the parade judges announced the traditional three award winners.

Next, the Mayor announced the start of a fourth annual award; this one to be given to the parade group who displayed the most holiday spirit. Mrs. Claus moved forward to the microphone and declared, "Selecting one single group to receive this wonderful award proved to be extremely difficult. With the judges' and parade organizers' support, I wholeheartedly resolved that every single person in attendance, whether marching in the parade or watching, deserves to have the Most Holiday Spirit award! You have all clearly demonstrated just how much you delight in this occasion and time of year, so give yourselves a round of applause for lifting the spirits of all who came tonight! Thank you one and all for inviting me to be a guest judge this year!"

The crowd responded with a hearty cheer and thundering applause, as Santa gave an equally hearty "Ho, Ho, Ho". He admired his wife for coming up with such a wonderful way to honor all the people of this quaint and lovely town. Such a tremendous showing of holiday spirit from one and all truly impressed Santa and touched his heart.

Then the countdown to light the Christmas tree began with the crowd chanting "three, two, one!" On the count of one, Santa and Mrs. Claus threw the switch and the tree suddenly lit up, shining brightly for all to bask in its glow.

Tinsel had seen the Christmas tree lighting ceremony up at the North Pole, of course, but this was something entirely new and wonderful! Suddenly though, he notices the reindeer seem up to something, so he decides to follow them. Any thoughts on what Tinsel observes?

Chapter 6: Post-Parade Fun
& a Pinch of Reindeer Mischief

Immediately after the Christmas Tree Lighting Ceremony, a line started to form outside the building across from the Courthouse and Old County Jail Museum. Children eagerly awaited entry into the John Barton Payne Building, now officially called "Gum Drop Square" for the rest of December. Volunteers escorted Santa to the specially decorated comfy chair placed in the section of the large room which had been decorated with hundreds of snowflakes and dozens of gingerbread house creations. As soon as the doors opened, the children rushed forward, eager to have their turn with Santa. He smiled and suggested, "Remember now, to be as patient as you can be so each one of you can visit with me." Santa began to engage with every child, listening to their wishes and assuring everyone that they were on the Nice List.

A photographer was there capturing the special moments for each family. The Gum Drop Square supervisor offered complimentary photos for Santa to add to his and Mrs. Claus' legendary photo album. Santa gladly accepted. "It brings so much happiness to Mrs. Claus and me when we look back at the children's faces, shining with excitement and pure joy," explained Santa.

As Santa was escorted to Gum Drop Square, Mrs. Claus touched Dancer's shoulder. "Dancer, earlier this afternoon, Santa and I found a lovely vintage clothing shop. I purchased a handsome tuxedo for you and the most darling dancing dress for me! The manager said she'd allow us to do a quick change so we can dance in style and comfort," revealed Mrs. Claus.

Meanwhile, out on Main Street at the Courthouse steps, the Silver Tones Swing Band was starting to play, while the Silver Belles sang along to the enchanting holiday music. A few experienced swing dancers were teaching basic swing dance moves to volunteers from the audience. Dancer, who, of course, was a highly experienced dancer, took Mrs. Claus' hand to twirl her onto the dance floor.

The crowd parted and watched in awe of Dancer's expert ability as he led his graceful partner around the floor. Momentous applause burst forth as the song ended, and Mrs. Claus' red velvet skirt swirled around her as she and Dancer took one last spin. As she blushed, Mrs. Claus quickly curtsied to Dancer and the audience.

Once more the band started to play, but now Dancer and Mrs. Claus

encouraged everyone to join them in the holiday fun. This time people of all ages and dancing abilities crowded the dance floor, smiling, and singing along to the cheerful holiday music.

After the second dance, Mrs. Claus uneasily said, "Dancer, my mischief-in-the-making meter is busily buzzing. I think we better go check on the other reindeer."

So, thanking the band and guests for a lovely dance, Mrs. Claus and Dancer went looking for the rest of the reindeer team.

Vixen was indeed getting into a bit of mischief as he tried to pull a prank on Comet and Cupid. The three reindeer had followed some local folks into the Old Jail on a private tour, but they trailed behind at one of the jail cells.

Vixen then coaxed his friends into the cell, closing the door on them! Comet and Cupid giggled nervously a bit, finding themselves inside a jail cell.

However, just at that moment Mrs. Claus appeared with Dancer and Blitzen! She gently, but firmly scolded Vixen, saying, "Why did you leave the other reindeer? You were supposed to stay together. Now, can you open that door, or do we need help from the North Pole Emergency Response Team?" Mrs. Claus watched Comet and Cupid exit the jail cell. "Now, that is better," continued Mrs. Claus, "Please stay together, preferably with me, so there is no more trouble tonight. Vixen, I know you think this is funny, but the real fun is out with all the people who are enjoying the amazing festivities!"

Then Mrs. Claus smiled and said, "I heard several folks reminiscing about how the Silver Tone Swing Band sounded so much like part of the USO Tours held when they served during wartime. I know you all are aware of the USO Tours produced around the world for the soldiers and sailors on deployment. The entertainers are proud to help support these men and women and keep up their morale while they are away from their families. Did you notice the military veterans who were honored during tonight's parade? That makes me want to go visit the Harvey L. Pearson Armory, to welcome home the soliders coming home from deployment."

"You know that means I need my cookies which I left in the back seat of Santa's sleigh! It is a good thing I made a batch just last night. First, Dancer and I also need to change out of our dancing outfits. Now, I expect the rest of you to wait quietly behind the shop for us," stated Mrs. Claus. After changing back to her formal dress and cloak, Mrs. Claus gave more directions.

"Alright then, Vixen, Comet and Cupid – to make up for your mischief this evening, I would appreciate it if you would go and take these beautiful outfits with you as you retrieve my cookie tins. You may leave the garment bags in the back seat of the sleigh. Please be discreet as you go and return, so you do not distract the crowd!" cautioned Mrs. Claus.

Vixen replied, "Mrs. Claus, we promise to be careful and will be back in a jiffy!" So, off the three reindeer flew, far overhead of the townspeople, back to the Fauquier Fairgrounds. There they found Mrs. Claus' special cookies and carefully delivered them to her in less than three minutes.

"Thank you for being so quick and careful!" said Mrs. Claus. "Let's go on over to the armory. I hear it is next to a place called the WARF which should be easy to find since it has a swimming pool and a skateboard park. I would like to show my respect to those soldiers and celebrate with their families."

Rudolph suggested they do a hop-skip to the armory so Mrs. Claus wouldn't have to walk across the intersection at Routes 29 and 211. So, Dasher knelt down to let Mrs. Claus sit on his back. Then he gently escorted Mrs. Claus to the armory with the rest of the team. There she greeted all those on duty and handed out her very special Christmas cookies.

"On behalf of Santa and the North Pole, we want to recognize each of you for your dedicated service and the sacrifice of time away from your families while on deployment. We try our best to help support your families on Christmas Eve, as they sacrifice being with you too," declared Mrs. Claus.

After thanking the soldiers for their service, Mrs. Claus and the reindeer decided to again hop-skip back over to Main Street. As they landed near the bakery with a delightfully old red truck, they enjoyed the brisk air with various musical groups set up at the Old Town Post Office and Courthouse steps. Mrs. Claus led the reindeer along Main Street, asking them to specifically take note of the intricately decorated shop windows.

"Wow! I guess we have been so busy having fun with all the parade activities and townsfolk that we didn't notice all the creative decorations in the shop windows," said Comet.

"I agree! I love showing off my nose for the children, but the decorations are also entertaining as well!" exclaimed Rudolph.

"Well, a big part of being on the Official Team is to engage with all the people you meet. I just wanted you to see the level of detail Old Town Warrenton puts forth to make this place a wonderful experience for Christmas season visitors," explained Mrs. Claus. "Santa and I have enjoyed this Christmas tradition of window gazing for over a hundred years!"

As the reindeer walked with Mrs. Claus, the farmer was still giving rides in his wagon, while his eager passengers joyfully joined in the caroling which seemed to be everywhere. The adults spoke of the farmer's incredible history of growing gorgeous Christmas trees, while the younger ones laughed with joy at seeing the horses pull the wagon.

Children ran back and forth with neon glow sticks and jingle bells, while the Warrenton Town Police officers carefully watched and smiled at all the holiday cheer. Rudolph allowed his nose to glow, which never failed to enchant children of all ages.

Later, after walking up and down Main Street, Mrs. Claus thought they should check on Santa at Gum Drop Square. "I am certain that Santa is enjoying his time visiting with all the children, but it looks like the event organizers are closing the line now. Let's go wait for Santa near the end of the line." There they mingled with the last of the families waiting for their turn with Santa, bringing an extra magical moment to the children who admired the reindeer.

Rudolph continued to let his famously red nose glow because he liked to show people how his nose had earned him a place on Santa's Official Team. While the other reindeer were amused at their youngest teammate, Comet decided to use his love of stargazing to point out several constellations to the waiting children.

Soon though, Santa finished visiting with the last child for the evening and joined Mrs. Claus and the reindeer on the sidewalk. Santa leaned over to his wife and shared, "Jessica, I heard several people talking about an amazing Live Nativity display happening tonight! You know how much it would mean to me to get to see the Living Nativity. I think maybe it is just down this hill, but we can ask someone for directions."

Just then, the Mayor of Warrenton walked over to the steps beside Gum Drop Square to meet up with Santa and Mrs. Claus. When the Mayor heard Santa mention the Living Nativity, he stepped over to them, explaining that there had been four churches who traditionally worked to set up a Living Nativity display. Some years the display was set up near the Courthouse, but this year it was at Eva Walker Park. The whole group walked down the hill to the park to view the amazing display, which had live animals as well as real people.

As they arrived, Santa heard one of the church leaders talking to a small group saying, "In the 3rd Century, Saint Nicholas started a tradition of gifts for children, showing the love of Jesus for all people. Many of the traditions celebrated in modern times originate from the ways Saint Nicholas helped so many children."

Santa declared to Mrs. Claus, "What a thoughtful explanation of how our tradition first began! Jessica, just look at all the effort and attention to detail that the church group has put into setting up this Living Nativity! This is truly wonderful to behold." As Santa always did when he came across a display with baby Jesus, he knelt down and bowed his head.

After a few moments, Santa slowly stood and quietly watched. Then, he observed a crowd forming around the scene. Santa and Mrs. Claus nodded to the reindeer and slipped quietly to the back of the crowd.

Tinsel followed Santa down to the park where he beheld a beautiful scene, broken only by the donkey's hee-haws. He knows he will keep this magical experience in his heart better than any of his photos could do. But – he realizes he has one big problem! How to get back to the sleigh?

Tinsel followed Santa down to the park where he beholds a beautiful scene, broken only by the donkey's hee-haws. He knows he will keep this magical experience in his heart better than any of his photos could do. But – he realizes he has one **big** problem! How to get back to the sleigh?

Chapter 7: Goodbye For Now!

Santa, Mrs. Claus, and the reindeer all gazed one last time at the marvelous Living Nativity scene. As they stood there, they soon realized the Mayor had his vehicle waiting at the edge of the park to drive them back over to the Fairgrounds.

Santa quietly gave directions to the reindeer: "Walk quickly over to the next street and fly back to the Fauquier County Fairgrounds. Make sure you get a quick drink of water and a snack while you wait for us." The reindeer team acknowledged Santa's instructions and left as inconspicuously as possible, to avoid making a disruptive scene.

Santa and Mrs. Claus joined the Mayor in his vehicle. As they drove away, the Mayor gratefully remarked, "Thank you, Santa and Mrs. Claus, for coming to our small but amazing town! You have made a special event all the more special for being here with us. The folks in attendance tonight have shared how they will never forget this experience!"

Mrs. Claus responded, "We are the ones who are truly thankful. Warrenton is an exceptionally charming town. Everyone here has given us a tremendous gift, sharing their holiday spirit and energy!"

Santa, echoing Mrs. Claus, said, "Thank you for your kind invitation! Mrs. Claus has a knack for knowing just where I should go during the Christmas season, and I have enjoyed myself immensely!"

At this point, they were now back at the entrance to the barn where the sleigh had been hidden. As they exited the vehicle, Santa and Mrs. Claus waved goodbye to the Mayor, suggesting he alert the crowds to watch for the sleigh on their way back to the North Pole.

Enthusiastically agreeing with Santa's request, the Mayor called his assistants as he rushed back into Old Town, where the news spread like wildfire throughout the remaining crowd.

Following Santa's instructions, the reindeer had used their lightning speed to dash from the park over to the Fairground. Back in the barn, the reindeer enjoyed some icy cold water and carrots. Meanwhile, as Santa spoke with the Mayor about the special flyover, the reindeer whispered their idea about a vacation to Mrs. Claus. "I had the same idea!" exclaimed Mrs. Claus. Bursting out laughing, Mrs. Claus quickly hushed herself so Santa would not hear. "Let me think about how to approach Santa and see what he thinks of a vacation in Fauquier County. For now, it's 'Operation Silent Night!'"

"What's all the fuss about?" asked Santa. "The Mayor is headed back to Main Street, so we need to get ready for departure. We need to focus because he is spreading the news about the special flyover as we head out of town." Santa ran the safety checklists to ensure he had harnessed the reindeer correctly and that Mrs. Claus had properly secured her seatbelt in the sleigh.

With everything and everyone ready to go, Santa radioed the Vint Hill TRACON announcing that SleighRider1 was ready for take-off from the Fairgrounds, with a small change in flight plan to fly over Main Street. After TRACON flight controllers granted flight clearance, Santa gave instructions to fly in slow-motion, so the children could see them as they drifted over the street.

As the sleigh approached the Courthouse steps, Santa tugged slightly on the reins allowing them to hover for a moment. Santa and Mrs. Claus waved at the awestruck crowd who stood cheering as they waved back. Parents quickly hoisted their young children up onto their shoulders to give them an even better view. The reindeer gaily tossed their heads as they maintained the sleigh in mid-air.

As everyone eagerly watched, Santa gave a hearty shout: "Merry Christmas to all and to all a good night! I will be back on the 24th!" Then he firmly shook the reins and called the reindeer by name: "Now Rudolph! Now Dasher! Now Dancer! Now Prancer and Vixen! On Comet! On Cupid! On, Donner and Blitzen!"

The crowd gasped as Santa's sleigh took off like a rocket, looking like a silhouette for a brief moment as they passed in front of the moon. The people marveled at how this had been a once-in-a-lifetime experience. This was one night that would be the talk of the town for ages to come.

Thank goodness, Tinsel managed to jump into Santa's bag! With a sigh of relief, Tinsel ponders how he will boast to the other elves about this amazing experience. How long do you think it will take before Tinsel's story makes its way to Santa's office?

Chapter 8: Great Minds Think Alike!

As they sped along back to the North Pole, Mrs. Claus smiled and glanced at Santa. He turned to look adoringly at his wife. "Jessica, my dear, thank you so much for all your help today. You always know just what I need, whether it be a little adventure to witness holiday spirit or reminding me how not to get my beard and suit messed up when I eat."

Laughing gently Santa continued, "I really do appreciate all you do for me, the elves and everyone you meet. You have such a caring heart! I am so glad we could go on this trip together. We make a spectacular team!"

Mrs. Claus blushed and replied, "Thank you, Kris! I am so glad I could accompany you on this wonderful little adventure. You know how much I love all that we do for children all over the world. There's nothing else I'd rather do!"

She paused and proceeded, "By the way, Kris, I had an idea I'd like to share with you. What would you think of coming back during our vacation season for a few days? The reindeer would like to return, as would I. There are so many wonderful places to see and things to do in Fauquier County."

Mrs. Claus resumed, "Not to mention, if we came back next December, we could check out the Christmas parades in Remington and Marshall! Fauquier County has some fascinating traditions at Christmas time and throughout the rest of the year, too."

Santa laughed so hard that his belly shook just like jelly. "Now why didn't I think of that?" he teased Mrs. Claus, "Actually, I had the same idea earlier today, and wanted to talk to you about it. We had such a brief glimpse of the people and places in Warrenton, but I believe we really should come back for a longer visit in our downtime late next spring. There are certainly places I know I would like to see such as the Fauquier Historical Society Museum, the Cold War Museum, Monroe Gold Mining Museum, plus so much more!!"

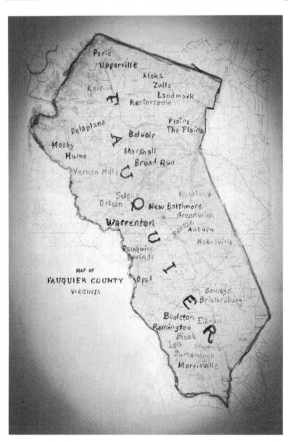

Then suddenly they looked at each other and exclaimed simultaneously, **"But first – Christmas!"** Santa and Mrs. Claus chuckled as they enjoyed their little inside joke.

After a moment, Santa continued, "Seriously, though, after we complete the Christmas Eve deliveries we can talk more about a vacation. Thank you, Warrenton, and Fauquier County, for a marvelous experience tonight! I can hardly wait for December 24th!"

Epilogue

Unbeknownst to Santa (or so Tinsel thought), a certain junior elf congratulated himself on his success at stowing away on the adventure to Warrenton! Tinsel honestly thought he had managed to hide himself on the sleigh without anyone noticing. He had taken his tiny digital camera (designed and produced by Santa's Workshop, of course) and now had hard evidence of his success. "Just wait 'til I show these pictures to the other elves!" Tinsel thought. "I will have the respect of all the elves! Maybe this will lead to other adventures!"

And yet…unbeknownst to a certain elf named Tinsel, Santa was well aware of what Tinsel had done! Once they were safely back at the North Pole, Tinsel would soon find out what happens to junior elves who get themselves onto the Naughty List.

Brief Background for Locations & People

Eva Walker Park: The lady for whom the park was named shared a home with husband, Robert, and their two daughters (Robyn and Sherrie), overlooking an empty field. Mr. and Mrs. Walker opened their home to children and youth and helped raise funds to improve Warrenton.After many years, Mrs. Walker succeeded in persuading the field's owner to donate the land so the children could have a place to play. Mr. and Mrs. Walker both had a tremendous impact on desegregation in Warrenton. In recognition of all Mrs. Walker did in her short life, the park was named in her honor.

Fauquier County Fairgrounds: County fairs have existed since the early 1800s and Fauquier County has hosted its own fair for decades. Exhibits, demonstrations and activities are spread out over the fairground's 10 acres. Competitions are held for prize-winning vegetables, baked goods, animals, and artwork. The Miss Fauquier pageants are also held at the fairgrounds each July during the 4-day annual event.

Green Building Murals: The three murals were commissioned by William Green and designed/painted by Stewart B. White. Mr. Green built the structure intentionally leaving out any windows, to allow for the murals. These were designed with the goal of encouraging people to think of all the ways all people were affected by the Civil War.

Harvey L. Pearson Virginia Armory: The armory is actually a Virginia Readiness Center for the Virginia National Guard. This armory is named after Harvey L. Pearson who served in the United States Air Force during WWII. He flew 50 missions and returned home to Warrenton, where he served 32 years as Clerk of Court. The Delta Company, 3rd Battalion, 116th Infantry Regiment is based here. The soldiers just completed a deployment in November 2022!

John Mosby House: This house had served as a museum for John Mosby who was a prominent citizen in Fauquier and Loudoun counties during the Civil War. His home is a Warrenton landmark. It is currently a private residence, not open for tours.

John Barton Payne Building: Each December the John Barton Payne Building gets transformed into a winter wonderland with gingerbread house displays, snowflake designs and Santa's chair. The Fauquier County Public Library system currently operates the building. The JBP Building serves the county as a community hall, hosting a variety of events including being the site for Gum Drop Square. Naming the building for John B. Payne is Warrenton's way of honoring the man who served as US Secretary of the Interior for President Woodrow Wilson and provided the funds to build the first permanent library in Warrenton.

Old Fauquier County Courthouse: Known as one of the iconic buildings in Warrenton/Fauquier County, the courthouse is actually the 4th courthouse to stand in this Main Street location. Previous courthouse structures were destroyed by fire. It currently functions as the General District Courthouse. Residents and visitors alike can still listen to the beautiful bells and see the town's Christmas tree each December.

Old Jail Museum: The jail is celebrating the 200th anniversary in 2023 of its 1823 building. The jail, however, was fully operational as early as 1808 until it closed in 1966. Visitors to the Fauquier Historical Society and Museum can view exhibits on John S. Mosby, "Extra Billy", local women's suffrage movement and local artifacts, along with checking out several areas of the old jail.

Old Town Athletic Campus: OTAC was founded in 1996 by Kim and Mike Forsten. They wanted to give back to Warrenton, by helping people of any age and fitness ability. Originally, OTAC was located across from the Warrenton Cemetery, and moved to its current location off of Walker Drive to expand into larger space for their new types of fitness programs.

Red Caboose: The red caboose at the western end of the Warrenton Branch Greenway marks the endpoint of the old railroad which closed down in 1989. The Piedmont Railroaders partnered with several people, including the Fauquier Trails Coalition and later on, the Friends of the Caboose to bring this project to life and maintain the caboose for all to enjoy. The Norfolk Southern Railway graciously donated a N & W #51884 caboose, which was refurbished by the Piedmont Railroaders. The Fauquier Parks & Recreation hold ope house events several weekends each year for children and families to view the interior of the caboose and hear volunteers share the history of the caboose and railroad.

Silver Tone Swing Band: The band originated in 2012 and performs music from the 1940s-1950s "Big Band" era, as well as more recent music, at venues all over the area. Several times a year the band can be found in Warrenton. They are happy to teach swing dance to anyone who comes to their concerts and have singers who also specialize in this era of music (Sinatra, Andrews Sisters and more).

Check back soon to see the list of our release dates and upcoming books from Tinsel Thyme Press, LLC., Website: www.tinselthymepress.com

Tinsel Thyme Press

Current titles available:

The Making of Santa

Beyond the Beard: The Collective History of Santa Claus

'Twas the Night Before Christmas in the County of Fauquier

'Twas the Night Before Christmas According to Santa

Santa Visits the Old Fauquier Jail

Made in the USA
Columbia, SC
15 September 2023

22920339R00030